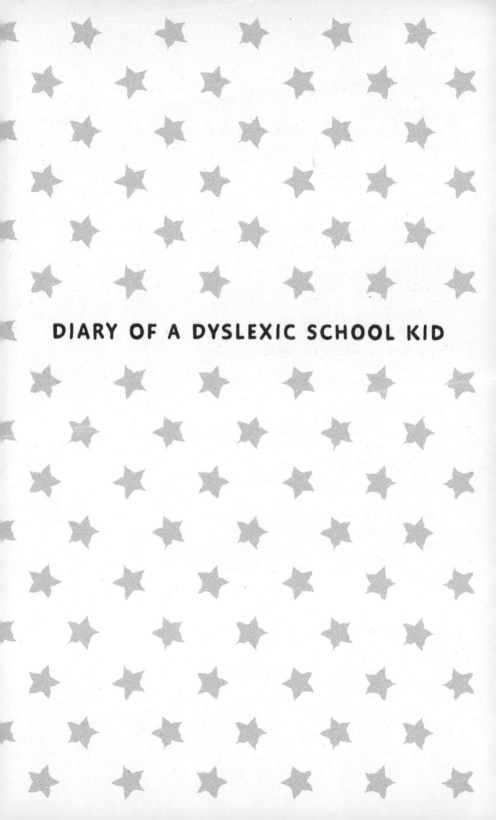

DIARY OF A DYSLEXIC SCHOOL KID

DIARY OF A DYSLEXIC SCHOOL KID

Alais Winton
and
Zac Millard

ILLUSTRATED BY JOE SALERNO

Jessica Kingsley *Publishers*
London and Philadelphia

First published In 2020
by Jessica Kingsley Publishers
73 Collier Street
London N1 9BE, UK
and
400 Market Street, Suite 400
Philadelphia, PA 19106, USA

www.jkp.com

Library of Congress Cataloging in Publication Data
Names: Winton, Alais, author. | Millard, Zac, author. | Salerno, Joe,
    (Artist) illustrator.
Title: Diary of a dyslexic school kid : Alais Winton and Zac Millard ;
    Illustrated by Joe Salerno.
Description: London ; Philadelphia : Jessica Kingsley Publishers, 2020. |
    Audience: Grade 4 to 6.
Identifiers: LCCN 2019001205 | ISBN 9781785924422
Subjects: LCSH: Dyslexia--Juvenile literature. | Dyslexic
    children--Education--Juvenile literature. | Dyslexic children--Family
    relationships--Juvenile literature. | Diaries--Juvenile literature.
Classification: LCC LB1050.5 .W4948 2020 | DDC 371.91/44--dc23 LC record
available at https://catalog.loc.gov/vwebv/search?searchCode=LCCN&searchArg=
2019001205&searchType=1&permalink=Y

British Library Cataloguing in Publication Data
A CIP catalogue record for this book is available from the British Library

ISBN 978 1 78592 442 2
eISBN 978 1 78450 814 2

Printed and bound in Great Britain

For Hannah,

I could not have got through this year without you
and Zac wouldn't be here without you.

We both love you to the max.

For all dyslexics, we get it and you are not alone.

Acknowledgements

Mega thanks to Zacharia Millard for co-writing this book with me.

Thank you so much, Joe Salerno, for your amazing illustrations that bring this book to life.

A big thank you to Hannah Rackham who does so much to help both authors.

Thanks also to Simon Green for communicating emails to my co-author, occasional lifts for writers' meetings and support with various technical nonsense.

A huge thanks to all of my clients and ex-clients who have shared their stories and their views about certain aspects of the book. I really value all of your contributions, your honesty about your personal experiences and the hard work you all put in to what we do – I could not be more proud.

To Amy Lankester-Owen, my editor, for ongoing support and lengthy phone conversations.

To Emily Badger for always helping out and everyone else at JKP who make my books a reality.

Thanks to Geoff Winton for setting up my new computer so I could finish writing the book.

Thanks to Alex Essex for getting me online again so I could send the manuscript to my editor.

Thanks to all my friends, family and client families who have all supported me practically and emotionally during a difficult year.

Finally, thank you to anyone else who helped and supported me with the writing of this book.

AUTHOR'S NOTE

This book is about the life of a dyslexic teenager: Cal.

We thought it was important to include deliberate spelling, grammatical and punctuation mistakes to show how Cal might write.

Like many dyslexics his mistakes are inconsistent and can appear random in nature.

We have also used slang at times as Cal is a young person.

Please do not copy Cal's mistakes.

If you would like to improve your spelling and punctuation please see: *Fun Games and Activities for Children with Dyslexia* (Jessica Kingsley Publishers, 2018) or *The Self-Help Guide for Teens with Dyslexia* (Jessica Kingsley Publishers, 2015) by the same author, Alais Winton.

Many thanks, the authors – Alais Winton and Zac Millard.

This book belongs to...

This ~~dairy~~ *diary* belongs to Cal – that's me, it's short for Callum but everyone calls me Cal.

Mum gave me this book to write in so I can write better 'cos i'm ~~dyslectic~~. *dyslexic*

She said if I write in it for a whole year she will buy me something super awesome.

The good thing is I can put whatever I want in it...

I just opened this page again and someone has been correctin my spelling, sooo someone has been reading this... Mum!!!!

I spoke to Mum and told her this is top secret!! She has promised not to read it anymore if I ask her to help with my spelling. I said OK.

September, Sunday

No school today – woop, woop. I have to write something before I can go do what I really want to do – like go out on my scooter or play Minecraft.

I really hate writing 'cos its hard and I'm not good at it, so I'm gonna do a list of stuff I hate and stuff I'm into...

STUFF I HATE

Homework!!!

Reading out loud in class – just why, people????

Bullies.

Getting lost.

Being late.

Forgetting stuff.

Loosing my stuff.

Getting into trouble for stuff that is so not my fault!!.

School – worst subjects:

English   Maths
Science   History

STUFF I'M INTO

Drama – I'm a superstar and I'm gonna be proper famous one day.

I.T. – THAT'S COMPUTERS (if you are <u>still</u> reading this mum, even though I told you not to).

Design Tech – I get to make super cool stuff in that class.

Riding my scooter – obvs.

My x-box.

Getting away with stuff that mite have been my fault.

Adventures.

Art.

People I like.

My mum (when she's not shouting at me or my dad!).

Doing good at something.

TV.

Sick – I have written loads and it wasn't all bla, bla, bla and me fake writing, so I am going out on my scooter now and won't be home till it gets dark – laters!

Monday 9th September

First day at a new school today.

I am eleven now so I have to go to what we all call 'big school'.

I wish I didn't live in the UK, I wish I lived in America then I wouldn't have to change schools, plus they have really cool stuff in America.

I live in Wales, it's full of mostly sheep and it's well boring – yawn!!!

Anyway my big day starts like this I get up well early and put on the gross uniform.

My uniform is grey and itchy and it doesn't even fit properly.

I'm ment to grow into it!!!!! How harsh is that?

It takes me ages to find my school stuff and I'm starting to stress that I will miss the bus.

When I'm well stressed I go and wake mum up to say I'll prob need a lift.

Really don't wanna be late on my first day.

Mum is super grumpy and says school starts tomorrow and I have to go back to bed.

I'm happy I don't have to go to school today but gutted I got ready for like no reason whatsoever.

I go downstairs and watch telly but as quiet as I can get it so mum will think I went back to bed.

When mum does finally get up she still looks grumpy and shouts at me for still being in my uniform.

I hate the stupid thing but I couldn't be bothered to get changed.

I told her I was wearing it in.

She said I would mess it up and had to change at once!!!

Tuesday 10th September

First day of school – for real this time!!!!

I sooo do not wanna go but there is no way Mum will let me stay home on the first day.

Even if I was proper dying she'd make me go.

There is only one seat left when I get on the bus.

I had to sit next to a smelly kid – yuk.

When I'm on the bus I suddenly realise I've left my ruler at home and I need it for maths.

Too late now.

I would tell the bus driver it's an emergency and we need to turn round, right now but I can't think of a reason to tell him that I won't get into trouble for.

I mean if I say my mum is dead or something like that he's gonna know as soon as we get there and tell my mum what I said – sooo not worth it.

I have a few good mates at school who were at my other school and meet a new kid who seems okay.

Break times are good I like hanging out with my mates and we have a laugh about the new teachers.

The new teachers are mostly super strict and well old and boring.

I got lost on my way to the first lesson after lunch 'cos I couldn't find the science block.

It was miles away from the cafeteria!

All the classrooms are labelled in blocks a–e, but there is no block c – sooo random!

So anyway I got muddled up and went to the English classroom by mistake.

I was late for science and got a bad mark for it.

Then I got into trouble in Maths for not having my ruler.

One more bad thing and I will get detention on day one!!!

Tried to look as if I knew what was going on and that I was super interested for the rest of the day.

It went okay and I didn't get into any more trouble.

But when the buses came Josh shouted to me that he hoped I hadn't turned into a super swat.

Everyone heard and stared at me – so not cool Josh!

Wednesday 11th September

I just noticed how stupid the spelling of Wednesday is, I mean what's that d for? If you said it out loud it would be Wed nes day, but I asked mum and she says it does have a d in it.

Had French today at school.

French!!! What's the point of learning French? I'm never going to France. I don't know any French people and I can't even write proper English yet.

Who comes up with this stuff? It's crazy.

Thursday 12th September

Got lost in school again today, which made me a bit late for everything!!

I reckon I will probly work out where all the classrooms and stuff is just before I leave in about five year's time.

Had science today for the first time. Miss said we were all going to do a fun test to see what we already knew.

Tests are not fun!!!!

Only a teacher would think a test is a fun thing to do – they are so old and totally boring.

It turns out I didn't already know very much apart from my name and the date.

Friday 13th September

We had drama today and I was like totes amazing...

We had to do this thing called impro that is just making stuff up.

Sir said I was really good at it and that I have a creative mind.

I wish mum had the money to send me to a proper drama school.

Then I could end up in The Big Bang Theory – I'm going to practise my American accent now.

Saturday 14th and Sunday 15th

No school!

No homework!!

Not raining – Sick.

Went out on my scooter both days.

Wanted to go the skate park in town but mum said no.

Will keep asking 'bout the skate park till mum finally gives in.

Monday 16th – Friday 20th

This week has been sooo mega boring, that I don't even wanna write about it.

I get up stupidly early.

Go to school.

Come home have dinner.

Go to bed.

Totes yawnsville!!!!

Monday 23rd

Had my first English class today.

We got given some Shakespeare and had to write it in the way we talk now.

Everyone else finished before me.

I didn't have a clue what it meant.

Reading gives me a headache anyway, but this was well difficult.

Shakespeare is soo lame, I hate him!

Tuesday 24th

Double Maths today – arrrgh!

We were doing long division.

Why can't I just use my phone calculator to work it out?

That's what anyone would do if we wern't in school!

Maybe the teachers too old to know that theres an app for that?

I wonder if I should tell him, probly not teachers hate it when you know stuff they don't.

Wednesday 25th

French followed by games today.

In French we had to read about some boy called Pierre.

He has a stupid name and does boring stuff like going to the shops with his aunt.

In games I got muddled up 'cos of the French and kept saying wee (oui) instead

of yes, everyone thought it was well
funny, apart from Sir who told me off for
being rude.

I didn't know what he was on about I was
only talking French...

Thursday 26th

Got my test back in Science
today, its covered in red
pen I can't even read
what Miss has put.

I only got 4%.

Even though the teachers all keep saying
that at the moment our scores aren't
important or anything to worry about I still
have to see Miss after class about it.

Miss said I need to try harder, but I did try!

I just didn't get it!!!

Friday 27th

Drama is the best!

We did a short play today.

I only had one line but I don't mind 'cos I find it hard to learn lines or read and walk at the same time.

I did an amazing death act.

Sir said that it was the longest and most dramatic death he has ever seen – go me!!!

Monday 29th

I have been at my dad's house for the weekend and I forgot to take this with me.

We were so busy that I prob wouldn't have had time to write anything anyway.

I also forgot to pack my English book, so I got into trouble for not having it in school today.

I told mum when I got home in case the teacher's tells her at parents evening and she went mental.

I told her that it was down to her that I live in 2 different places. She sent me to my room!!

It is well unfair.

Tuesday 30th

Had English again first lesson today – why do we have to do so much English?

Got given homework.

I have to read about Shakespeare and then write some stuff about him.

Why do I need to know about stupid Shakespeare – he's well dead.

Wednesday 1st October

Made a new mate today.

His names David and he seems sound.

I tried to talk him into doing my English homework.

He said – 'no way!!!' He hates English too.

Thursday 2nd

Tried to get mum to do my stupid homework but she said she is well busy and stressed.

I went to my room and tried to read the stuff about Shakespeare.

After half an hour I knew it weren't happening, and started to get salty (angry).

I heard a ding on my phone, it was Snapchat.

David was saying look at Jordan's story.

He posted a picture of my face on a monkey and said 'I bet this monkey is smarter than Cal'.

Then I totally lost it, ripped my homework up and threw it out the window.

Friday 3rd

Had to give my homework in today.

Was given a bad mark for not giving it in and I have to do it in detention on Monday.

Mum's not gonna be happy but I swear down, I did my best!

Saturday 4th and Sunday 5th

It has been raining most of the weekend!

Plus I am totally grounded after throwing my homework out the window on Thursday night.

I had to help mum tidy the house.

Also I can't go on my games console for a week!!!

Luckily mum hasn't worked out I've got some games on my phone or she would've taken that off me as well.

Monday 6th

Detention sucked big time!!!!

Still couldn't do stupid homework.

So I just wrote random about Shakespeare living in the olden days.

When people wore different clothes and everything smelt really bad, 'cos they have proper toilets – yuk!!!!

Tuesday 7th

In History today Sir asked me how many wives did Henry the 8th have and I said 'more than he needed'.

Everyone apart from Sir laughed.

Sir told me the right answer which is six.

So one for every day of the week, apart from Sunday, when he probably had a rest from his wives and went out with his mates instead.

I wasn't bothered about getting it wrong until I heard Jordan behind me chanting 'Duh brain' over and over, super quiet but loud enough for me to hear!!!

Wednesday 8th

Nothing happened today!! Literally nothing!!!!

Thursday 9th

I was telling Josh in the cafeteria about some new stuff I'm adding on Minecraft.

I'm building a train track, it is gonna be soo sick, its unreal.

Anyhow I was getting excited and waving my arms about a bit and I knocked my glass over.

Unluckily Jordan was on the next table and when he saw it he shouted out: 'Hey Cal, how come your parents let you out when your such a duh brain?'

Everyone laughed.

I shouted 'I'm not a duh brain – you are!'

But it was a lame come back and no one laughed.

39

Friday 10th

Last day of school before half term – a whole
week off from this place – mega woop.

It was all going good at first.

I was looking forward to going home and
then packing for my Dads who I am gonna
stay with for the week.

Then at break time Jordan was with some
other boys in our class and he waved me over.

I thought he was gonna say sorry for what
happened yesterday.

We used to be mates in junior school.

He whispered something to me but I couldn't
hear it so I said 'What?' and then he went
'Oh, I just said stupid says what, and then
you said what, so you must be stupid!'

His mates thought it was well funny.

I just walked away.

Saturday 11th – Sunday 19th

No school for a whole week – yea!!

Monday 20th

It is my birthday today!!! – Woohoo.

I still had to go to school – which is the worst place in the whole world!

I still had to do my English class – which is the worst subject in the whole world!

When I got home mum was late back from work sooo I couldn't open my presents until

she got home which was pretty much my
bed time.

My Aunty looked after me while my mum
was at work.

She isn't my real aunty she's just a friend of
my mums who lives in the same street.

She's alright I guess but food was yuk and
she acts like I'm three years old.

So my birthday was not very Woohoo
after all.

Tuesday 21st – Tuesday 28th

Not much to say really.

School is still well boring and the work is
still well hard!!

Jordan keeps making sly little comments in class, saying I'm dumb and stuff but the teachers never hear him.

Soo he never gets into trouble, but if I say something back I always get into trouble.

Mum says she is pulling her hair out about how I act in class, but she looks like she still has loads of hair.

Wednesday 29th

Parent's evening. Mum is still having a go 'cos I lost the letter about this.

We are running late 'cos she can't find her keys. It is well stressville.

The hall is rammed when we get there.

I want to go see the drama or art teachers 'cos I'm good at those and the queues are short but mum says we have to see English, Maths an Science.

The queues are well long...

The English teacher says I need to improve my focus and read more. I hate reading!!!

The Maths teacher says I need to put in more effort and practice improper fractions and simultaneous equations – say what????

The Science teacher says we are a good group this year – even mum was confused by that comment.

Then mum dragged me over to see a woman on a dyslexia table, I didn't wanna talk to her it was well embarrassing!

Friday 31st October

OMG!! It is Halloween,
and on a Friday – so
I can go out trick or
treating.

David is coming to
call for me in like ten minutes.

My costume is like so epic, you would not
believe!!!

I'm a zombie spaceman – how cool is that?

Saturday 1st November

I had to come home early last night.

We saw Jordan out with a gang of his
mates and they started shouting at us and
throwing eggs.

Mum is still in a mood about the smell and the mess from getting hit by eggs – like it's my fault!!!

Jordan proper sucks now!!!

I can't believe we used to be mates.

Tuesday 4th

I missed the bus home today, so I had to walk.

Jordan and his new mate spotted me when I was about half way home.

They cornered me against a tree and took turns hitting me and spitting on me.

Eventually Jordan said 'I can't be bothered to hit him any more right now'.

Then he looked at me lying on the floor and said 'I hate you, you are a freak'.

They ran off laughing.

It took me proper ages to get home 'cos everything hurt so much.

Mum went nuts when she saw me but said I didn't need to go to hospital.

Wed 5th
. . . .

I get to stay off school today 'cos of what happened yesterday – woop, woop!!

That's the good thing, the bad thing is I don't get to go bonfire night, tonight for the same reason.

Mum says she will phone the school today, she is well annoyed.

Thurs 6th

The school told mum that 'cos I got beaten up on my way home and not in school that its nothing to do with them!!!

So I have to go in today or I will get a bad mark for being off.

Also mum says she can't take any more time off work to look after me.

I don't need looking after, I'm like twelve now.

Why can't she just leave me at home with the x-box???

Friday 7th

I am jus tryin to stay as far away as possible from Jordan and his mates right now.

I'm well miserable!!!

Mon 10th

I was at my dad's this weekend.

I told him about Jordan 'cos he kept asking why I had a face like a smacked bottom.

He wants to know where Jordan lives so he can go and kick off at him and his parents.

I said I wasn't sure so he said he would ring mum.

She will not be happy about this!!!

Monday 1st December

Mum says if I don't start writing this again I won't be having any xmas presents.

She says I haven't done a stroke of work for months.

I stroked the arm of the chair to show that I had but she didn't think it was funny (even though it properly was!!).

She doesn't get it! There's a new game out called Fortnite – everyone is playing it and talking about it and I'm good at it!!!

Tuesday 2nd December

Jordan was whispering stuff in History today.

I have been staying out of his way at lunch and break times, but I can't avoid him in class.

He sat behind me and said 'This isn't over Dumbo', 'I'm gonna get you'.

I ignored him like mum said.

I didn't tell Sir 'cos then I'd get a rep as a snitch and everyone would hate me!

Plus I'd have to prove it to Sir, like I'm gonna have a spy cam and get secret footage to show him!!!

Friday 5th December

We had to do a practice paper in Maths this morning.

I hadn't studied for it 'cos I have a life!!

It was super hard,

I think I did really bad.

Drama was awesome as always and I was great at acting being a robot.

Saturday 6th December

Today was like the WORST day ever.

I was doing my robot act so my mum could benefit from my great acting.

She said it was irritating her so she sent me to the shop to get a few things.

When I got there I saw Jordan and like my whole school hanging out by the shop.

Jordan gave me this sly look as I walked toward him.

When I went past him, I turned around and he pulled my trousers down.

I was soo EMBARRASSED!!

I punched him.

Then I quickly pulled up my trousers and ran off.

I know it was wrong to hit him and I'm supposed to tell on him.

I'm meant to act like a scardy cat.

Mum will go ape when she finds out about this.

WHY ME????

Wednesday 10th December

Someone has dropped me in it big time!!!

I got home from school and mum said
'Come here Cal, I want a word with you.'

I knew this meant trouble, and I was right.

One of the parents of someone watching
what happened on Saturday rang my mum
at work to tell her what happened.

Mum said even though Jordan should not
have done what he did there is no excuse for
hitting him.

She said I need to be more like Gandhi.
I said 'What like drink a cup of herbal tea
and walk away?'

She told me not to talk back to her.

I am grounded for two whole weeks and no x-box or phone or computer for two weeks as well.

I am gonna be sooo bored!!!

Thursday 11th December

BORED!!!!

Friday 12th December

SOOO BORED!!!!

Saturday 13th December

MEGA BORED!!!!

Sunday 14th December

ARRRRGH!!!!!!

Monday 15th December

David found me at lunch today.

He said 'I gotta talk to you, right now'.

Like it was some big drama.

It turns out Jordan has started picking on some other kid.

Its all over facebook – but I didn't see it 'cos I'm still banned from facebook.

This other kid Simon has been telling everyone, his mum, teachers, other kids so now everyone is calling him sissy Simon and snitch Simon.

Oh man, his life is gonna be hell!!!

Wednesday 24th December

It's Christmas Eve and I'm finally allowed all my stuff back.

I was well happy and wanted to go on the x-box straight away.

Mum said I could have half an hour while she gets ready 'cos we have to go to some stupid carol thing.

I don't mind singing but I hate tryin to read the words and sing at the same time.

I find it hard enuf to read when I'm not doing anything else.

Reading and singing together is just Random and weird.

Thursday 25th December

Christmas day!!!

I got up at 6am 'cos I can't wait to open my presents.

Hope I get the hover board I have been begging for all year.

It would be really cool if mum also got the hint about me needing a new plasma television.

Also hope I get a new headset for the x-box, mine is well old.

I went downstairs to watch some random stuff on television, but mum got up like five minutes later and sent me back to bed.

She said it was way too early to be up, clearly this was not true 'cos I was up!!

I had to wait forever before I could get up.
I couldn't go back to sleep so I spent ages
just staring at the ceiling till I heard mum
moving about downstairs.

When I did go down I had to wait ages to
open my presents 'cos mum said she needed
help in the kitchen.

When I complained that I was not her slave
she said 'Christmas dinner isn't going to
cook itself'.

I wish it would, I told her that's what
she should have asked Santa for, she
just laughed.

Most of my presents were rubbish; shower
gel, pants, socks, a very old dvd and loads
of school stuff.

My face was proper hurting from fake
smiling all afternoon.

My last present was the hover board, I love it and I can't wait to go on it.

Friday 26th December

Boxing day...

I was made to play lame family games all day!!!

All I wanted to do was go on my hover board but mum said it was family time, but she meant just me and her really.

Scrabble was the worst, she kept telling me I couldn't have my word 'cos it was spelt wrong.

Scrabble sucks!!!

Wednesday 31st December

New Year's Eve...

Woop, woop I get to stay up till midnight –
totally sick...

It's now 10.30pm and I am
totes bored.

Mum has been watching some
romantic comedy for hours and
I'm not allowed to go to my room.

Mum said she wanted me to keep her
company, but she isn't really even talking
just keeps drinking wine and crying at
the film.

I'm gonna text David when I think she
won't notice, just to see if he is doing
anything better...

Monday 5th January

First day back at school after the hols and I totes don't wanna go.

Even though I don't think Jordan will bother me anymore, at least for a bit.

School is just so lame.

Tuesday 6th January

Got English again today and I just don't get it.

We have to learn Adverbs and Adjectives, Nouns and Pronouns????

More like Greek than English if you ask me.

Also I thought a preposition was when you asked someone to marry you, not another word for <u>on</u> or <u>under</u> or something.

Thursday 22nd January

I haven't wrote in this for a while 'cos I have been doing Fortnite as soon as I get home.

I proper love it.

Luckily I don't think mum has noticed.

She is well stressed about work at the mo.

She says she never seems to have any money or time off.

Is she working for free or what?

Friday 23rd January

We had our practice Maths paper back today.

The one we did before Christmas.

I got 8% (so like 8 out of 100).

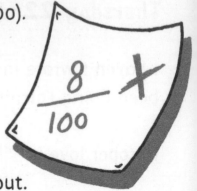

Mum is gonna be soo mad at me.

I don't know if I should tell her or wait for her to find out.

Monday 26th January

I acted well miserable all weekend.

Mum kept asking me what was wrong.

I just said I didn't want to talk about it.

Then when I got home from school today I told her I was really down about my Maths result.

When I had told her what I got I asked if she was annoyed at me.

She said 'Oh Cal, I'm just disappointed'.

She asked how I was doing in English.

I told her I was doing okay, I didn't wanna make her even sadder.

Friday 30th January

So the great news is we're going do a play.

I'm gonna be in it for def.

The bit that sucks is we're gonna do Shakespeare.

What I hate about Shakespeare is:

He didn't have a speare.

His name is hard to spell.

He makes all his characters talk weird.

His stuff is well old and out of date.

He has written mostly about love – yuk!

Some people say that he didn't write it either, he might have nicked it off someone else!!!

Tuesday 10th Feb

I always try to write Feb instead of the long version of this month 'cos it's such a hard word to spell.

Why didn't they make days and months easy to spell when they made them up.

And make the hard ones to spell words we would hardly ever use like ballroom.

You only have a ballroom if you're well posh

and only girls and old people watch ballroom dance – not me yuk.

Wednesday 18th Feb

Mums birthday is today!!!

I almost forgot like I did last year.

What with mum being so grumpy all the time and my exam results not great, forgetting would not be good.

I wrote it on a piece of paper, that I lost.

I wrote it on my hand and that washed off.

Then I figured out how to put an alarm about it on my phone – I'm super smart really.

I got her some stinky perfume.

I thought it smelled rank – but mum loved it.

Thursday 26th Feb

COLD – Brrrr!!!

Friday 27th Feb

WELL COLD – Brrrr!!!

Saturday 28th Feb

FREEZING – Why doesn't mum turn the heating up????

Sunday 29th Feb

Leap year – but still FREEZING!!!

Monday 1st March

ST DAVID'S DAY

I live in Wales so we celebrate this David dude who has been well dead for ages but was important to Wales or something.

What it means for me is I have to go to school looking like an idiot.

When we were young we all had to dress up proper Welsh and get our photo taken as a class.

Now I just have to have a leak pinned to my jumper.

Still well embarrassing and someone shouted 'Oh look Cal the vegetable is wearing a vegetable', when I walked into class.

I didn't see who said it so I made out like I didn't hear it.

Tuesday 10th March

Something well random happened today.

My teacher said I had to go to room C12 at break time.

I thort I was well in trouble about something but couldn't think what.

When I got there a boy who is older than me said 'Hi, I'm Joe, you must be Cal'.

I was like 'Yeh, thats me'.

Then he told me he was my anti bullying mentor.

I don't know what a mentor is but Joe is well cool.

He said that this group called BulliesOut came into school and gave them training so that they could look out for younger kids.

Joe asked if I had seen any bullying or been bullied at school and I was like well 'Duh, course.'

Joe says I should tell a teacher what happened to me and I said no way, I'll get beaten up for being a snitch.

Joe said he would be looking out for me, and that we'd tell one of the cool teachers and that it was up to the school to stop it happening 'cos its their job.

I don't know if that would help but I really like Joe and he showed me an online thing about acting like you don't care when bullies say mean stuff.

'Cos if you act like you don't care the bully gets bored.

Def gonna try that next time I get grief off someone.

Monday 21st March

I haven't written in this for ages 'cos mum said if I help her out around the house I don't need to do any writing for a few weeks and she would help me with my English homework.

Good deal or so I thought.

We fell out over the helping out.

I did the washing up in the wrong order – I didn't even know washing up had an order.

I put all the bedding on inside out mum said she would have to do it all again.

I don't know why. No one sees the bedding except us.

I also knocked over mum's pottery dog when I was dusting, she was annoyed.

Mum should have been happy about the broken dog it was hideous!!!

Thursday 24th March

Mum came back from work in tears today.

I asked her what was wrong and she just said 'There's no use crying over spilt milk'.

So I poured a bit of milk on the worktop to see if that would help.

It didn't help; she just got more upset and sent me to my room.

I was just doing what she said – parents are soooo weird.

Friday 25th March

Today is the last day of school before the Easter Hols.

I have 2 whole weeks off – woop woop.

Monday 11th April

First day back at school after the hols and I soo do not want to go.

Easter was awesome!

I still got loads of Easter eggs 'cos mum and

dad both reckon I'm still young enough to get them.

I think they both wanted to get me more than the other one did.

Dad also got me a battle pass for my Fortnite game, so now I have a new skin. Having a new skin (player) is well cool.

My new one can do a funi chicken dance and have a pet in his backpack.

The best pet is the robot cat, it doesn't do much but it looks awesome.

It didn't rain loads like it usually does so I went out on my scooter most days.

I was well tired having to get up for school but mum jus kept saying 'You've had 2 weeks off, you should be fine, and when do I ever get a rest?'

Thursday 14th April

Had Science today or Ski ense as I call it 'cos it helps me spell the stupid word.

Honestly if I can't even spell what my subjects are called how am I s'possed to do well in them?

Miss said that we have to start thinking about the exam next month.

She told us we need plenty of time to revise.

Plenty of time to stress about it more like.

Only the kids that always do well anyway
didn't look freaked out at the end
of the lesson.

Will I get any marks for being good at
getting the Bunsen burner to work?

I didn't ask Miss, I was worried she might
say no.

Friday 15th April

OMG, the play is in like 2 weeks time.

I just know I'm gonna be awesome.

Also I will have loads of practice to do so
mum will have to know that I won't have
time to do loads of other work, like English
or tidy my room!!!!

Friday 22nd April

Just 1 week till the play.

We are doing Macbeth.

Weird thing is we're not allowed to say the name of the play in the theatre 'cos it's bad luck – random!

I play some dude that gets killed but then turns up as a ghost to like totes wreak a dinner party.

I'm well good and Sir said I would have had a bigger part if I could do the words easier.

But Shakespeare wrote well hard words to say.

It's all *doth* and *hast* and *saith*, why couldn't he talk normal???

Friday 29th April

BIG NIGHT – it's the ACTUAL, PROPER PLAY tonight – for real!!!

Mum is coming to see it.

I've already told how awesome I'm gonna be.

Dad said sorry but he can't make it – what could be more important than my first starring role???

I wish I had my own dressing room but Sir said we all have to get ready in the boys toilet – not the girls obvs.

Saturday 30th April

I'm well tired today.

We had to tidy all the chairs away after the play so got back home well late.

The play was sooo cool.

I didn't forget any of my lines. Mum said that she knows words are hard for me and she was super proud.

I'm gonna sign her copy of the programme today 'cos it will be worth a fortune when I'm famous!!!!

Monday 1st May

It is a bank holiday today.

I don't work in a bank, but I still get the day off school – woop, woop.

Fortnite here I come...

Tuesday 2nd May

Had English today.

We had to do revision 'cos we have an exam soon.

Revision means going over stuff I didn't understand the first time round and still don't get now!

It's well annoying.

Why can't we have exams bout x-box games, I'd totes SMASH that!!!!

Thursday 4th May

Science exam was today!!!

Miss said she hoped that we'd had lots of time to study.

Is she loco or what????

I've been way to busy being a cool actor.

I have tried to forget this was happening...

Think this may have been one of my WORST EXAMS EVER!!!!

Friday 5th May

I was really looking forward to Drama.

I wanted to act something cool to take my mind off exams.

But when we got there Sir said: 'You must all be tired from doing a play. I know I am. So I think you should all read quietly.'

Then he gave us some boring books about plot device and stuff.

Mega lame – I hate reading quietly.

Friday 12th May

School has been well boring all week.

Everyone is dead quiet and stressed bout the exams.

Even the teachers have stopped banging on about stuff they jus give us exam questions to look at to prepare.

This just stresses everyone even more!!!

Mum says that I have to spend all weekend studying 'cos the exams are next week.

My life is well unfair – how come she doesn't have to sit in her room studying all weekend???

I can't wait to be grown up so I can do what I want all the time.

Tuesday 16th May

ENGLISH EXAM – TODAY!!!!

Everyone (so like my teachers and my mum) have been saying I should just do my best.

Well guess what?

I did my best and I'm really not sure it will be good enuf...

The questions were well hard and I didn't have enuf time to read the stuff I was supposed to write about so I didn't even finish...

Friday 19th May

MATHS EXAM – TODAY!!!!

I think I did K.

Better than English anyhow.

Sir said we had all worked really hard this year and he was dead proud of us.

When he asked if there were any questions at the end of the exam I asked if he could put the thing about being proud on my exam paper when he marked it – he just laughed.

David said afterwards that Sir probably wasn't allowed to mark our exam that they send it to someone else.

How dumb is that?

Sir is the one who knows if it's right or not 'cos he told us in the first place...

Monday 22nd May

Another day off for a bank holiday!

I proper love May, it's awesome for random days off!!!

I am 'resting' 'cos I've had exams.

So mum is letting me laze around the house.

When she tells me to get dressed I just say but I'm well tired after my exams and she lets me off.

I don't think this will last.

Tuesday 23rd – Friday 26th May

Rest of half term!!

Super cool!

I knew that I had yesterday off, but I didn't know I had a whole week off school 'cos it's half term.

David messaged me to meet up and I was like: 'dude I'll see you in school'.

He was like 'no way man we're off for the week'.

Gonna go in to town tomoz to hang out with David, if mum lets me.

Tuesday 30th May

HISTORY EXAM TODAY!

I thought we had like done all our exams, but oh no there's more!!!

History was hard 'cos I couldn't remember loads of names and dates and stuff.

I really wanted to write *all these people are well dead why does any of this matter?*

I didn't put that 'cos Sir would've been well mad.

I did make some stuff up though.

We had to name a load of Welsh dudes in a black and white photo.

I didn't know any of them so I just put down all the famous Welsh people I'd heard of like Tom Jones.

Tom Jones prob wasn't even born when the photo was taken and he would have been singing if it was him, but the teachers said we shouldn't leave any questions blank...

Wednesday 31st May

FRENCH EXAM TODAY!

The first question was PARLEZ VOUS FRANCAIS? (Do you speak French?)

So I just put Um NON (NO) and didn't really think I needed to carry on after that.

I did draw some pictures of Pierre doing stuff in France.

Maybe mum will let me drop French next year when she sees how mega pointless it is.

I NEVER want to go to France they eat snails – Yuk!

Super gross!!

Thursday 1st June – Friday 16th June

Sooo the last two weeks have been mega dull! Dull, dull, dull.

Now that the exams are over we have to read stuff in class about what we will be doing next year.

I hate reading!!!!

I'm always well behind everyone else.

Also I don't understand even half of what we're ment to be reading.

What's the point?

I think the teachers just can't be bothered to teach us right now.

They all look done in.

Saturday 17th June

Was going to stay with my dad for the weekend, but he just rang to say he can't see me.

Something came up – what does that even mean.

I am well grumpy about it.

Mum is trying to tell me that I will have just as much fun at home with her – yeah right!

She'll be telling me how lucky I am next and if I say I'm bored she'll tell me to tidy my room.

Monday 19th June

I turned up to English early, for the first time today.

I got lost at lunch time and ended up at the English classroom.

When I got there my teacher was looking at a holiday magazine.

It's weird to think of teachers going on holiday – like there real people or something.

Tuesday 20th June

I got my Maths exam back today. I only got 19%.

I thought I did okay.

I'm guessing mum won't be happy.

Thursday 22nd June

We were given back our Science exam paper today.

I got 31% so way better than I thought I'd done.

Miss said that we all did really well.

We still had to go over the questions we got wrong though.

Monday 26th June

ENGLISH EXAM RESULT – 8%

Mum will never believe I tried hard with this result.

I proper did my best – for real and look what happened.

This is mega lame.

I think mum might actually cry when she hears my result.

Wednesday 28th June

I got my French exam mark today.

I got 3% – worst result EVER!!!

I soo need to drop French!!

The teacher put a comment on it to say I should only draw pictures in an Art exam.

My pictures would have been no good for Art as they were all of Pierre.

Also we don't even have exams for Art now, because it won't get us a proper job or something.

Teachers say well random stuff sometimes.

Saturday 1st July

Mum said I could have tried harder in my exams especially French.

She said that I did okay in Science which is good but I have to work much harder at everything else.

'Cos of my French result I have to help mum tidy and clean the house all weekend – nightmare!

I don't deserve such horrible punishment...

It's only French.

Tuesday 4th July

If I lived in America today would be a really cool day with like parties and fireworks and stuff.

Sadly I live in Wales so it's not cool and instead I got my History exam paper back.

I got 22%.

My teacher put on it that if I learn things and stop making stuff up I might do better next time.

Obvs not impressed with genius idea of just naming all the famous Welsh people I know...

Friday 7th July

Mum had a meeting with the school today about my exam results.

She said that they know I'm dyslexic 'cos my other school told them but they want to do their own test on me.

I told mum that sounded lame and I didn't want any more tests.

Mum says they want to see how bad it is so I can maybe get extra time in exams next year, or even have someone to read or write for me in an exam.

I thort that mite be cheatin, but mum swears it totes isn't and that if I need some help I should get it.

Go mum!!!

Saturday 8th July

Went to my dad's this weekend.

Woop, Woop!

Dad said not to worry about my exam results.

He says what you learn after you finish school is more important.

I'm not sure what he was on about but I went along with it 'cos he seemed happy.

Monday 10th July

Mum said it mite be a good idea to get me a tuter next year to help me after school.

Mum says it will cost money but maybe dad could help out.

'But he always says that hes skint' I told her.

Mum said that her friend Seren told her about something called time banking.

I said her friend was off her head 'cos you put money in banks not time, duh!!!

Mum got grumpy with me n told me off for being rude.

She says time banks are a way for people to swap their time n what they are good at for something else.

I still didn't get it, mum tried to xplain she said dad could do like an hour gardening for someone n then get me a teacher for an hour.

It sounds well hard but I guess if it works its a cool idea.

Friday 14th July

Last day of term.

Totally awesome!

I've got six weeks off school.

Here we come x-box, scooter, seeing my mates, freedom!!!!

Further Reading

HELPFUL ORGANISATIONS

Bullies out (advice and workshops on anti bullying):
https://bulliesout.com

Dyslexia information, support and training:
www.bdadyslexia.org.uk

How to stop a bully video:
www.brooksgibbs.com

BOOKS

Alais Winton (2015) *The Self-Help Guide for Teens with Dyslexia*. London: Jessica Kingsley Publishers.

Alais Winton (2018) *Fun Games and Activities for Children with Dyslexia*. London: Jessica Kingsley Publishers.

Kate Collins-Donnelly (2018) *Starving the Exam Stress Gremlin*. London: Jessica Kingsley Publishers.

Michael Panckridge and Catherine Thornton (2017) *Be Bully Free*. London: Jessica Kingsley Publishers.

Fun Games and Activities for Children with Dyslexia

How to Learn Smarter with a Dyslexic Brain

Alais Winton

Illustrated by Joe Salerno

Full of fun, practical games and activities accompanied by charming cartoons for children aged 7 to 13 with dyslexia, this book makes learning easy and entertaining. Written by a dyslexic tutor for dyslexic students, the tips are embedded in first-hand experience and will inspire and motivate any reader to aim high.

The Self-Help Guide
for Teens with Dyslexia
Useful Stuff You May Not Learn at School
Alais Winton

Written by a dyslexic college tutor for dyslexic students, this book contains a wealth of tips and advice to aid successful learning. With ways to improve reading, writing, numeracy and organisational skills, this book offers solutions to common problems and will empower you to help get yourself through your teen years!

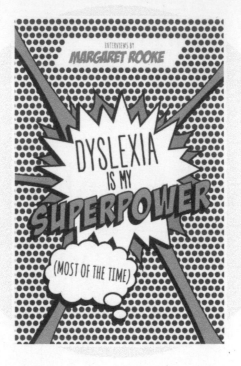

Dyslexia is My Superpower (Most of the Time)

Margaret Rooke

Forewords by Professor Catherine Drennan and Loyle Carner

Containing over 100 in-depth interviews with school children and young adults living with dyslexia, this collection depicts the significance of confidence and self-esteem in propelling children with dyslexia to achieve personal success. The children supply their own illustrations, along with a handy hints guide and their own advice to educators.

The Illustrated Guide to Dyslexia and Its Amazing People

Kate Power & Kathy Iwanczak Forsyth

Foreword by Richard Rogers

An engaging visual explanation of dyslexia, what it means and how to embrace it. Vibrant images and simple text depict what dyslexia is, along with helpful tools for learning and examples of skills and professions best suited for people with dyslexia. Includes tips for success, additional games and learning resources.

Be Bully Free

A Hands-On Guide to How You Can Take Control
Michael Panckridge and Catherine Thornton

Seeking to empower children who are bullied, this book presents a wide range of common bullying scenarios, before giving practical suggestions on how the recipient can take control in these situations. Written in a young adult fiction style, this is an essential resource for children who are experiencing bullying.

Starving the Exam Stress Gremlin

A Cognitive Behavioural Therapy Workbook on Managing Exam Stress for Young People

Kate Collins-Donnelly

When exam time comes around, the exam stress gremlin is in his element, feeding off your exam fears and anxieties. This workbook teaches you how to starve your gremlin by learning to cope with exam stress. Full of fun activities based on cognitive behavioural therapy, it is the ideal resource for supporting young people aged 10+.